D1259938

MULEY-EARS
Nobody's Dog

To the special boatboy
Who introduced me to
The special dog
Who owns a special house
On the isle of Jamaica

MULEY-EARS
Nobody's Dog

By MARGUERITE HENRY

Illustrated by WESLEY DENNIS

RAND McNALLY & COMPANY

Chicago · New York · San Francisco

A

Library of Congress Catalog Card Number: 59-5359

On the sunny, sunny, turtle-shaped isle of Jamaica there lives a dog whose name is Muley-Ears.

He is a strapping, deep-chested fellow with a coat of many colors—white and black and brown, with a patch on his shoulder as yellow as a banana. The natives say the shaggy whiteness comes from his grandmother, an Old English Sheep Dog, and the blue-black is the mark of his German Shepherd grandfather. There are tales, too, of an Irish Setter aunt and an Alsatian uncle and litters of mixed-up cousins.

But Muley-Ears does not look mixed up at all. He has great dignity.

His ears are the most magnificent part of him. They are simply abnormous! They stand up straight in the air, as if they were wired. In fact, when he sights a friend, or a fish, he pricks them so sharply they almost meet overhead. And that, of course, is how Muley-Ears came by his name.

For years, not counting one month, he has gone along happy as a clam at high tide. The whole beach is his playground. With his hackles high and his nose low, he stalks the never-ending waves as they break upon the shore. Barking fiercely, he plays a game of pounce with the creatures tossed up by the sea—the sand hoppers, the fiddler crabs, and the squid. Some he eats at a gulp; others he chases back into their hidey holes.

And when the sun fades into the bigness of night, then he and his moon shadow leap into the air for moths and bats, and the fireflies that are called Peenie Wallies.

Muley-Ears belongs to nobody. Even so—except for one month—his life has been full of fun and frolic. Everyone on the beach knows him and greets him with a "Hi, fellow," or "Hi, Muley." Or sometimes they use his full title of Muley-Ears.

And what's more, he does have a home. It's a friendly house, just a quick scramble up his very own trail through the jungle of palms and breadfruit trees. Its windows are screenless for jumping in and out, and its bare floors have been polished by many sandy feet, including his own.

This house of his is a For-Rent house. Every full moon or so, a new family arrives . . . with children swarming up the steps, carrying snorkels and fins, cameras and picnic baskets. Muley-Ears appoints himself *their* dog until they move out.

It is a fine arrangement. He doesn't get lonesome, and he keeps them from being lonesome for the dog they left behind.

With all the comings and goings, Muley-Ears is busier than a water bug. He makes it his job to show the boys and girls his favorite haunts—the dark cave where clouds of bats hang upside down, the river's bank where oysters grow on trees, the rocky ledge where lizards play skitter-tag.

He latches onto each new family as tightly as a barnacle fastens itself to the hull of a boat. If his people go rafting, he goes rafting. Whee, what fun shooting the rapids!

How the wind tickles his big ears as the current sweeps the bamboo raft through rocky ravines and gorges right down to the sea!

Along the shores browned Jamaican children, all elbows and knees, dance like puppets on a string. Gaily they blow their piping whistles at Muley-Ears. Their mothers, bent over piles of washing, look up laughing and wave sudsy shirts and shorts at him.

Oh, rafting is great!

By lunchtime his belly is all lean and empty. He can hardly wait for his family to choose their picnic spot on the beach, can hardly wait for them to open the food hamper. Always there are choice bits for him to share—sometimes cold lobster, or nubbins of roast pork, or codfish fritters. Or even a bone to work on!

When lunch is over, his people often snooze in a nearby fern thicket. Then he snuggles down alongside them and snores louder than the best.

Later when they go swimming, of course he goes swimming. He carries their towels and sand pails. He fetches balls and sticks for them.

And in return, they carefully search through his coat for mean, miserable ticks and quickly pluck them out.

Afterward, they all sit facing out to sea, watching the birds and boats go sailing by. Muley-Ears wriggles in very close to the children, not minding their damp bathing suits at all. Bursting with love, he just shares his wetness, batting them with his happy, soppy tail.

Whatever his family does, Muley-Ears does too. But one night a week, instead of being a tag-along, he shows *them* what to do. He insists on leading them to the docks where the bananas are loaded. Each time he enjoys it all over again . . . the torch flames dancing like sheets of lightning, but no thunder coming after; the glistening dark women shuffling from trucks to barges, stamping, swaying to their own singing.

In high spirits he frisks alongside them. He moves much faster than they do. After all, he has no heavy bunch of bananas to carry on his head.

Then on Saturdays he takes his people to the big outdoor market. While they are shopping he sniffs up and down the rows, enjoying the exciting smells, and the little handouts from the fishmongers.

If he upsets a huge tray of fruit with his busy tail, nobody seems to mind. "It's just our Muley-Ears!" And they laugh as they pick up the scattered limes and mangoes.

Going home on the twisty road, Muley-Ears often stops to rub noses with a nodding donkey.

"Jump up, boy!" the children shout. "Match your ears to his! We'll take your picture."

And up he goes, onto the donkey's back. Perched there between the loaded side baskets he poses big-chested and proud, while the cameras click.

Life is good!

But one month when the moon was new, a scowling man, a man with no family at all, moved into the For-Rent house. Muley-Ears was puzzled as he watched him come puffing up the path. He carried only an airline zipper bag. No cameras. No inner tubes. Not even a snorkel.

He was built like a pigeon, pompous and rounded in front; he even walked pigeon-toed.

This man didn't talk. Not to himself. Not to anyone. He didn't even talk to Muley-Ears! He only threw sticks and stones at him, but not for fetching.

From the very first it was plain to see he *just did not like company* . . . four-legged or two.

Think of it! The man didn't even own a picnic basket! He took his lunch down to the beach in a flimsy box tied with a thin string.

And what a glutton he was! He could eat a great hunk of sausage, a whole crayfish, and a loaf of rich sweet banana bread *all by himself.*

He didn't seem to understand that a dog came with the house, and that of course it was his job to feed him.

At first Muley-Ears stood nearby, lips drooling, eyes imploring. He watched sausage disappear, then fish, then bread.

But no crumb came his way.

Something was very wrong! Not one of his families had ever behaved so strangely.

How could he show the man the way people were supposed to act? He tried his best pleading. Sitting up on his haunches he begged, he barked sharp and clear, he offered to shake hands, first one forepaw and then the other.

For answer the man picked up a gnarled root and heaved it at Muley-Ears.

Then, at last, the dog gave up. He turned tail and wandered forlornly up the beach.

As the month dragged by, he grew thinner, and sadder. He kept alive on skimpy rations—little ticky-ticky fish, and minnows and mullets from the river. Once a week he went to market, but market days were far apart, and the few scraps from the fishmongers only teased his hunger.

A great lump of loneliness grew heavy inside him, and his once magnificent ears drooped. He began to hate the fat, fat man and the bulging box of unshared lunch.

He tried visiting nearby inns for friendship and food, but it just wasn't the same as having his own private family. Besides, almost all inns had special well-fed dogs who took full charge of leftovers. They wanted no help from hungry strays.

"You get off our property!" they growled. "On your way, you skinny snooper!"

Muley-Ears might have wasted away, except that one morning his luck turned. A fisherman's trap caught on a sharp edge of coral, and one by one the fish escaped through a hole in the wire.

He snapped them all up. Mmmm, they were plump and tender!

For the first time in weeks his stomach was stretched tight. Happily, and like the gentleman he was, he wiped his mouth in a fern bed. Then he lolled and rolled, rubbing his back in the sand.

It was sticky warm that day with no on-and-off-shore breezes. So when at noon the man waddled down to the beach, he did not eat at once. Instead, he carefully set his lunch box in the shade of a sea-grape tree. Then he went swimming. Of course he didn't really swim; he just floated.

Muley-Ears was no longer hungry, but from sheer dog habit he pounced on the unguarded lunch and hauled it away. Without opening the box at all, he buried it in the sand far up shore. There might well be other days when he'd have no fisherman's luck.

After a while the man came dripping out of the sea, shaking the water from each ear. He was hungry as a hungry alligator. Now for his lunch! He made a bee-line for the tree. But the lunch was gone—sausage, string, box, and all. There was only a smoothed square place in the sand.

Where in the world was it?

First he looked skyward. Had some bird swooped off with it? Some heron or pelican, perhaps?

Then he looked around and about him. Suddenly he bent double, staring at pawprints in the sand.

"Why, that sneaky thief!" he sputtered under his breath. "He can't get away with this!"

Waddling very fast, he followed the tracks. But the tide was coming in—lapping, lapping, washing the pawprints away.

Now, for the first time, the man spoke aloud. He raged. He roared. He bellowed like a bull.

"Where's my lunch, you robber!" he shouted to the small figure in the distance. "Where is it? Where!"

He was so busy shaking his fist at Muley-Ears that he stubbed his toe against something poking up out of the sand. It was the corner of a box. His lunch! He made a grab for it and angrily tore the box open.

Everything was there! That dog had not stolen so much as a crumb.

"I just can't believe it!" the man muttered. "I just can't believe it!" He looked long and hard at Muley-Ears, who was waiting far up the beach—watching, listening.

Suddenly the man felt a prick of shame. Red-faced, he pulled his pants on over his wet suit and climbed slowly, thoughtfully, up to the house.

For all the rest of that day he stayed inside. Through the window Muley-Ears could see him pacing up and down.

What was he doing in there? Why didn't he come out?

Once or twice he stood at the window with a look half puzzled, half cross, but his gaze went far out to sea.

Muley-Ears, too, felt strangely bothered. No matter how unfriendly the man had been, he was still living in his house.

So that night he did not sleep on the beach as usual. He waited for all the lights in his house to blink out and then crept into the clump of lilies just below the bedroom window. He was out of sight, yet so close he knew every time the man turned in his sleep. The night seemed never-ending. He watched the moon and the evening star slip down the sky into a pocket of the Blue Mountains. He listened to the man's breathing and to the gentle stirrings of the night breeze.

Only toward morning did he sleep.

The sun slanting into the lily bed nudged him awake. He waited around a while; then, hearing no sounds from the house, he had a good yawn and stretch and trotted down to the beach for a swim.

He saw nothing of the man until noon. When he did appear, Muley-Ears had to look twice.

Was this a different person?

So many things about him were changed. Even his walk. Instead of waddling down the path, he strode. In place of the old paper box he carried a generous-sized lard can.

As he settled himself in the shade of the sea-grape tree, he took off the lid and whistled coaxingly.

Cautiously, one step at a time, Muley-Ears crept forward—nose questing, ears at attention, all senses alert. He wanted so terribly to be friends.

But was the man really trying to be friendly? And could the man be trusted?

He sniffed the wind. He sniffed again, more deeply this time. There was no mistake. It *was* chicken. Fried chicken!

His lips drooled as the man carefully peeled the meat off the drumstick. Then with accurate aim he tossed the whole chunk to Muley-Ears, who caught it in mid-air.

It was delicious! Buttery and salty and tender. None of his other families had ever done better. All fears forgotten, Muley-Ears trotted up to the man, and there on the beach the two creatures sat side by side, chomping happily.

"You know, boy," the man spoke, and his voice was as different from yesterday's voice as sugar from salt. "You taught me a lesson, running off with my lunch and not eating a bite of it."

The big ears flicked, asking for more talk.

"I've been a stubborn old fool," the man went on. "For weeks you've tried to give me love and friendship, and I couldn't see it. I didn't even share my lunch with you.

"Y'see, boy, I never had much to do with dogs in the hotel back home. Matter of fact, guess I've never done much sharing with anybody.

"But this!" and he nodded toward the leftovers of their picnic lunch. "This is fun! Even if you are only a dumb critter. You'll pardon the expression," he added with a wink.

Muley-Ears, brown eyes shining, winked right back. His paw came down on the man's knee, and for sheer joy his tail swept a great happy arc in the sand.

And so, for the rest of his holiday, the man lived in this new way on the sunny, sunny, turtle-shaped isle of Jamaica. And each day he grew more content.

Together dog and man walked, and rafted, and explored the beaches and river banks. Muley-Ears showed his friend all the tucked-away things that had pleased his other families—the dark cave where clouds of bats hang upside down in the daytime, the old lizard with special suction pads on his feet for running around on ceilings, the oysters growing on trees. Together they hunted big green turtles to be made into soup. Muley-Ears even showed the man how to dog-paddle.

And always, always the big lunch was shared.

When the new moon rode high again, it was time for the man to leave. Over and over, that last morning, he invited Muley-Ears to fly home with him to the United States. But *of course* he couldn't go!

A new family with snorkels and fins and cameras and picnic baskets was climbing the path to his house.

PRINTED IN U.S.A